This Walker book belongs to:

_____

_____

This book is loosely based on an actual event: the first and only
attempted theft of the Crown Jewels, which took place on 9 May 1671.
To find out more about the truth behind this tale, please visit:
www.hrp.org.uk

First published 2014 by Walker Books Ltd, 87 Vauxhall Walk, London SE11 5HJ
in association with Historic Royal Palaces, Hampton Court Palace, Surrey KT8 9AU

This edition published 2015

10 9 8 7 6 5 4 3 2 1

© 2014 Historic Royal Palaces & Walker Books Ltd

This book has been typeset in Garamond

Printed in China

British Library Cataloguing in Publication Data: a catalogue record for this book is available from the British Library

ISBN 978-1-4063-6069-1
www.walker.co.uk

REX
AND THE
CROWN JEWELS ROBBERY

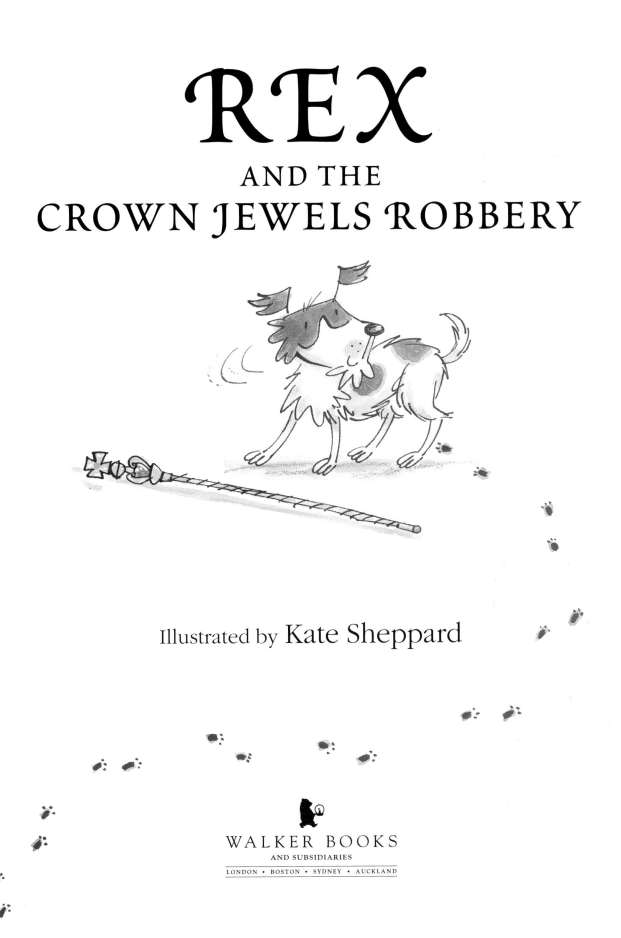

Illustrated by Kate Sheppard

WALKER BOOKS
AND SUBSIDIARIES
LONDON · BOSTON · SYDNEY · AUCKLAND

If you go to the Tower of London, you'll see signs that say NO DOGS ALLOWED. But there is a dog – a very scruffy dog – who lives there, right at the edge of Tower Green. His name is Rex.

Just look at him! He lollops along without a care in the world. His tongue is always hanging out of his mouth and he can never resist the smell of a juicy bin.

One Tuesday, Rex spotted a litter bin he'd never seen
before. Mmm, he thought. Delicious. It was just his
kind of bin – dirty and stinky and overflowing
with rubbish. He jumped right in
and wriggled around.

He dug down further,
and further,
and then he started falling.

He tumbled and turned
and twisted around,

until he hit the ground with a ...

THUD !

In a daze, Rex got to his paws and looked around.
Something was different. Everyone was wearing
funny clothes. It was as if he'd gone back in time!
But before he could explore, his nose began to twitch.
He could smell something wonderful – juicy, delicious
and really meaty. So he decided to find it.

Rex followed the smell into an old tower.
Something shiny caught his eye:
a hat, a ball and a stick, all made of gold.
Those dog toys look nice, he thought,
and he jumped up to take a closer look.
"Halt in the name of King Charles the Second!"
came a growl.

Rex spun around and saw a snooty-looking
dog holding a juicy steak.
"Can I have some?" asked Rex, his mouth dribbling.
"NO!" barked the dog. "And get away from there!
I am Cavalier, Guardian of the Crown Jewels.
How did a scruffy dog like YOU get in here?"
Before Rex could answer, the door creaked open.

"QUICK, HIDE!" barked Cavalier. "It's the Jewel Keeper, and I've got his steak!"

The Jewel Keeper walked in with three men.
One was short, one was tall, and one was dressed
as a priest.

"I present to you … the Crown Jewels!"
said the Jewel Keeper.

The short man said, "Oooh. That's a nice stick."

"THAT is not a stick," said the Jewel Keeper. "It's a gold sceptre."

The tall man said, "I like that ball."

"THAT is not a ball," sighed the Jewel Keeper. "It's an orb."

"Can I try on that lovely hat?" said the priest.

"THAT is NOT a hat!" huffed the Jewel Keeper.

"It's the King's crown!"

As the Jewel Keeper turned
to show them the crown,
the priest hit him
on the head.

BOING!

"*I'm not a priest,
you're a silly fool.
My name is Colonel Blood
and I'm stealing every jewel!*"
sang the priest as he tied up
the Jewel Keeper.

The short man dropped the orb down his trousers.

The tall man started sawing the sceptre in half.

And Colonel Blood stuffed the crown under his cloak.

"Let's stop them," Rex growled quietly.

But Cavalier was frozen with fright.

Typical, thought Rex. I suppose it's up to me…

Rex leapt up and set the Jewel Keeper free,
but the thieves were getting away.
"We've got to go after them!" barked Rex.
"I'll stay here," whimpered Cavalier.
"Oh, no you won't!" boomed Rex.
With a yelp from Cavalier, both dogs raced off.
"Wait for me!" the Jewel Keeper gasped.

"Get him!"
woofed Cavalier
as they ran past
the White Tower.

"Stop!" cried a
Yeoman Warder
as they passed
Traitors' Gate.

"Faster!" barked Rex as they raced across the cobblestones.
But Colonel Blood stayed just out of reach.

Rex ran faster than ever.
Faster than Cavalier.
Faster than the Jewel Keeper.
Even faster than Colonel Blood.

With one final leap he flew through
the air and bit Colonel Blood
on the ankle. It was bony and
hairy and NOT AT ALL juicy.
But he didn't let go.

"Get off!" snarled Colonel Blood,
 dropping the crown. "I HATE dogs."
"Off with his head!" cried the Jewel Keeper.
"Not so fast," said Colonel Blood.
"I demand to see the King."

King Charles II was very cross.

"How dare you steal my jewels!" he shouted.

"I see my crown and my sceptre, but where is my orb?"

The short man pulled the orb out of his trousers.

"I was just keeping it safe, Your Majesty."

"I should throw you all in the dungeons," said the King, "but I'm feeling forgiving. If I set you free, do you promise to be good?"

"We promise," said Colonel Blood. "We'll be very, very, VERY good."

The King looked at the thieves, and the thieves looked at the King.

Rex held his breath.

"You are all scoundrels," said the King, "but I will give you
a second chance. You are free to go."
The thieves hurried to the door before he could change his mind.

"The Crown Jewels are saved!" cried the King.

"A million thanks to brave Rex! A king among dogs!"

King Charles gave Rex a collar that was as golden
and glittering as the Crown Jewels.

Pretty ... but I can't eat it, thought Rex.

Then, once again, Rex's nose began to twitch. He could smell something juicy and delicious, and he decided to find it. He barked "Goodbye!" and followed his nose until he came to a litter bin.

He jumped in and dug down further, and further, and then he started falling.

He tumbled and turned
and twisted around,

THUD !

and landed right
in the middle of Tower Green.

Rex looked around – everything was back to normal. He heard a familiar voice. "Rex! Dinner time!"
Did I imagine the whole thing? he wondered.

But then he saw something golden
and glittering reflected in a puddle.

Maybe he hadn't imagined it after all.